THOMAS and the Guard

by
The REV. W. AWDRY

SCHOLASTIC INC.

New York   Toronto   London   Auckland   Sydney
Mexico City   New Delhi   Hong Kong   Buenos Aires

Thomas the Tank Engine is very proud of his branch line. He thinks it is the most important part of the whole railway.

He has two coaches. They are old, and need new paint, but he loves them very much. He calls them Annie and Clarabel. Annie can only take passengers, but Clarabel can take passengers, luggage and the Guard.

As they run backward and forward along the line, Thomas sings them little songs, and Annie and Clarabel sing, too.

When Thomas starts from a station he sings, "Oh, come along! We're rather late. Oh, come along! We're rather late." And the coaches sing, "We're coming along, we're coming along."

They don't mind what Thomas says to them because they know he is trying to please Sir Topham Hatt; and they know, too, that if Thomas is cross, he is not cross with them.

He is cross with the engines on the main line who have made him late.

One day they had to wait for Henry's train. It was late. Thomas was getting crosser and crosser. "How can I run my line properly if Henry is always late? He doesn't realize that Sir Topham Hatt depends on ME," and he whistled impatiently.

At last Henry came.

"Where have you been, lazybones?" asked Thomas crossly.

"Oh dear, my system is out of order; no one understands my case. You don't know what I suffer," moaned Henry.

"Rubbish!" said Thomas, "you're too fat; you need exercise!"

Lots of people with piles of luggage got out of Henry's train, and they all climbed into Annie and Clarabel. Thomas had to wait till they were ready. At last the Guard blew his whistle, and Thomas started at once.

The Guard turned around to jump into his van, tripped over an old lady's umbrella, and fell flat on his face.

By the time he had picked himself up, Thomas and Annie and Clarabel were steaming out of the station.

"Come along! Come along!" puffed Thomas, but Clarabel didn't want to come. "I've lost my nice Guard, I've lost my nice Guard," she sobbed. Annie tried to tell Thomas, "We haven't a Guard, we haven't a guard," but he was hurrying, and wouldn't listen.

"Oh, come along! Oh, come along!" he puffed impatiently.

Annie and Clarabel tried to put on their brakes, but they couldn't without the Guard.

"Where is our Guard? Where is our Guard?" they cried. Thomas didn't stop till they came to a signal.

"Bother that signal!" said Thomas. "What's the matter?"

"I don't know," said his Driver. "The Guard will tell us in a minute." They waited and waited, but the Guard didn't come.

"*Peep peep peep peep!* Where is the Guard?" whistled Thomas.

"We've left him behind," sobbed Annie and Clarabel together. The Driver, the Fireman and the passengers looked, and there was the Guard running as fast as he could along the line, with his flags in one hand and his whistle in the other.

Everybody cheered him. He was very hot, so he sat down and had a drink and told them all about it.

"I'm very sorry, Mr. Guard," said Thomas.

"It wasn't your fault, Thomas; it was the old lady's umbrella. Look, the signal is down; let's make up for lost time."

Annie and Clarabel were so pleased to have their Guard again that they sang, "As fast as you like, as fast as you like!" to Thomas, all the way, and they reached the end of the line quicker than ever before.

Now flip the book over to start another Thomas & Friends adventure.

Thomas the Tank Engine & Friends

A BRITT ALLCROFT COMPANY PRODUCTION

Based on The Railway Series by The Rev W Awdry
© Gullane (Thomas) LLC 2002

Visit the Thomas & Friends web site at www.thomasthetankengine.com

ISBN 0-439-33847-6

12 11 10 9 8 7 6 5 4 3 2 1   2 3 4 5 6 7/0
Printed in the U.S.A.
First Scholastic printing, April 2002

This edition is available for distribution only through the direct-to-home market.

Old Iron

by
The REV. W. AWDRY

SCHOLASTIC INC.

New York   Toronto   London   Auckland   Sydney
Mexico City   New Delhi   Hong Kong   Buenos Aires

One day James had to wait at Edward's station till Edward and his train came in. This made him cross. "Late again!" he shouted.

Edward only laughed, and James fumed away.

"Edward is impossible," he grumbled to the others, "he clanks about like a lot of old iron, and he is so slow he makes us wait."

Thomas and Percy were indignant. "Old iron!" they snorted. "SLOW! Why! Edward could beat you in a race any day!"

"Really!" said James huffily, "I should like to see him do it."

One day James' Driver did not feel well when he came to work. "I'll manage," he said, but when they reached the top of Gordon's Hill, he could hardly stand.

The Fireman drove the train to the next station. He spoke to the Signalman, put the freight cars in a siding, and uncoupled James ready for shunting.

Then he helped the Driver over to the station, and asked them to look after him, and find someone to relieve him.

Suddenly the Signalman shouted, and the Fireman turned around and saw James puffing away.

He ran hard but he couldn't catch James, and soon came back to the signal-box. The Signalman was busy. "All traffic halted," he announced at last. "Up and down main lines are clear for thirty miles, and the Inspector's coming."

The Fireman mopped his face. "What happened?" he asked.

"Two boys were on the footplate; they tumbled off when James started. I shouted at them and they ran like rabbits."

"Just let me catch them," said the Fireman grimly, "I'll teach them to meddle with my engine."

Both men jumped as the telephone rang; "Yes," answered the Signalman, "he's here . . . Right, I'll tell him.

"The Inspector's coming at once in Edward. He wants a shunter's pole, and a coil of wire rope."

"What for?" wondered the Fireman.

"Search me! But you'd better get them quickly."

The Fireman was ready and waiting when Edward arrived. The Inspector saw the pole and rope. "Good man," he said, "jump in."

"We'll catch him, we'll catch him," puffed Edward, crossing to the Up line in pursuit.

James was laughing as he left the yard. "What a lark! What a lark!" he chuckled to himself.

Presently he missed his Driver's hand on the regulator . . . and then he realized there was no one in his cab . . .

"What shall I do?" he wailed, "I can't stop. Help! Help!"

"We're coming, we're coming."

Edward was panting up behind with every ounce of steam he had. With a great effort, he caught up, and crept alongside, slowly gaining till his smoke box was level with James' buffer-beam.

"Steady, Edward."

The Inspector stood on Edward's front, holding a noose of rope in the crook of the shunter's pole. He was trying to slip it over James' buffer. The engines swayed and lurched. He tried again and again; more than once he nearly fell, but just saved himself.

At last—"Got him!" he shouted. He pulled the noose tight and came back to the cab safely.

Gently braking, so as not to snap the rope, Edward's Driver checked the engines' speed, and James' Fireman scrambled across and took control.

The engines puffed back side by side.

"So the 'old iron' caught you after all!" chuckled Edward. "I'm sorry," whispered James, "thank you for saving me." "That's all right." "You were splendid, Edward."

Sir Topham Hatt was waiting, and thanking the men warmly. "A fine piece of work," he said. "James, you can rest, and then take your train. I'm proud of you, Edward; you shall go to the Works, and have your worn parts mended."

"Oh! Thank you, Sir!" said Edward happily. "It'll be *lovely* not to clank."

The two naughty boys were soon caught by the Police, and their Fathers walloped them soundly.

They were also forbidden to watch trains till they could be trusted.

James' Driver soon got well in the hospital, and is now back at work. James missed him very much, but he missed Edward more, and you will be glad to know that, when Edward came home the other day, James and all the other engines gave him a tremendous welcome.

Sir Topham Hatt thinks he will be deaf for weeks!

Now flip the book over to start another Thomas & Friends adventure.